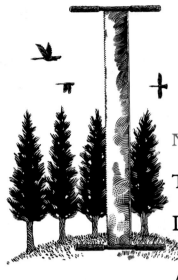

N THE FAR NORTH WOODS, WHERE THE

TREES GROW TALL, THERE WAS A

LUMBERJACK NAMED OLEE SWENSON.

All day long he and the other lumberjacks cut

down trees in the forest. "TIMBER!" they shouted

as each tree crashed to the ground.

~ *Olee Swenson* ~

~ The Hodag ~

A HUGE CREATURE WATCHED THE LUMBERJACKS AS they worked. It had the head of an ox, feet of a bear, back of a dinosaur, and tail of an alligator. It was forty feet tall, and its eyes glowed like fire. It was the HODAG! The Hodag looked mighty scary, but the lumberjacks were not afraid. They knew that the Hodag was their friend. A long time ago, he had helped them get rid of a mean boss man.

"LOOK!" CALLED OLEE SWENSON, POINTING to a patch of ripe blueberries. ❖ "Yum, yum!" roared the Hodag. "Save some for me!" Blueberries were the Hodag's favorite food. ❖ "We will," promised Olee Swenson. "But first we must cut down this tree." ❖ "Let me help," offered the Hodag. He crossed the clearing, his giant steps making the ground shake. Then the Hodag swished his scaly tail from side to side, and, CRASH, the tree came tumbling down. ❖ The Hodag settled down to feast on blueberries, crunching whole bushes in his giant jaws. While he ate, the lumberjacks plopped plump berries into their lunch pails. ❖ "We'll make pies for supper tonight," they said.

SOON THE SUN DROPPED LOW IN THE SKY. It was time for Olee Swenson and the lumberjacks to go back to the lumber camp. As they walked through the forest, they saw some men pitching tents around a campfire. ❖ "We are looking for the terrible Hodag," the men said. "We want to catch him and take him to the zoo. Have you seen him?"

"OH YES," OLEE SWENSON SAID. "The Hodag has the head of an ox, feet of a bear, back of a dinosaur, and tail of an alligator. His jaws are so big that he could eat you in one bite."

❖ Olee Swenson knew that the Hodag would never hurt anyone, but he was hoping to scare the men away. He didn't want their friend to go to the zoo.

~ The Animal Catchers ~

THE ANIMAL CATCHERS DID NOT SEEM WORRIED.
"Can you tell us where the Hodag lives?" they asked. ❖
"Look on the other side of the forest," said Olee Swenson.
"Maybe you will find the Hodag there." ❖ "We'll go there
tomorrow," they said. ❖ The lumberjacks smiled. They knew
that the Hodag never went to the other side of the forest. For now
he would be safe. ❖ Back at the lumber camp, the lumberjacks
prepared supper. ❖ "The Hodag would not be happy at a zoo,"
said one man. "The forest is his home." ❖ "Yes," said another,
"and we would miss our friend." ❖ "I must find the Hodag,"
said Olee Swenson, "and tell him to watch out."

THE HODAG'S DEN WAS DEEP IN THE FOREST. "Anybody home?" shouted Olee Swenson. ❖ "Here I am!" roared the Hodag. His fiery eyes glowed in the dark, and clouds of white smoke puffed out of his nostrils. ❖ "I have bad news," said Olee Swenson. "Some animal catchers want to take you to the zoo." ❖ "OH NO!" cried the Hodag. "I am too big for a tiny cage, and what would I eat? Wild blueberries don't grow in the city." ❖ "You must hide in your den," said Olee Swenson. "Then the animal catchers won't find you."

~ *"Oh no!" cried the Hodag.* ~

~ *"Did you find the Hodag?"* ~

THE NEXT EVENING, THE LUMBERJACKS SAW THE animal catchers again. They were covered with mud. "Did you find the Hodag?" the lumberjacks asked.   ❖   "No," said the animal catchers. "We went uphill and down, over a stream, around a lake, and through a swamp. We did not see the Hodag at all."   ❖   "Maybe the Hodag has left the forest," suggested Olee Swenson.   ❖   "We know that he is here," said the animal catchers. "We saw his footprints. Tomorrow we'll follow them back to his den. Then we'll catch him for sure."

THE LUMBERJACKS WENT BACK TO SUPPER.
"How can we stop them this time?" they asked. ❖ "I have an idea," said Olee Swenson. ❖ After dark the lumberjacks left the lumber camp. They tiptoed past the animal catchers' tents and walked deep into the forest. ❖ The lumberjacks found the Hodag and told him their plan.

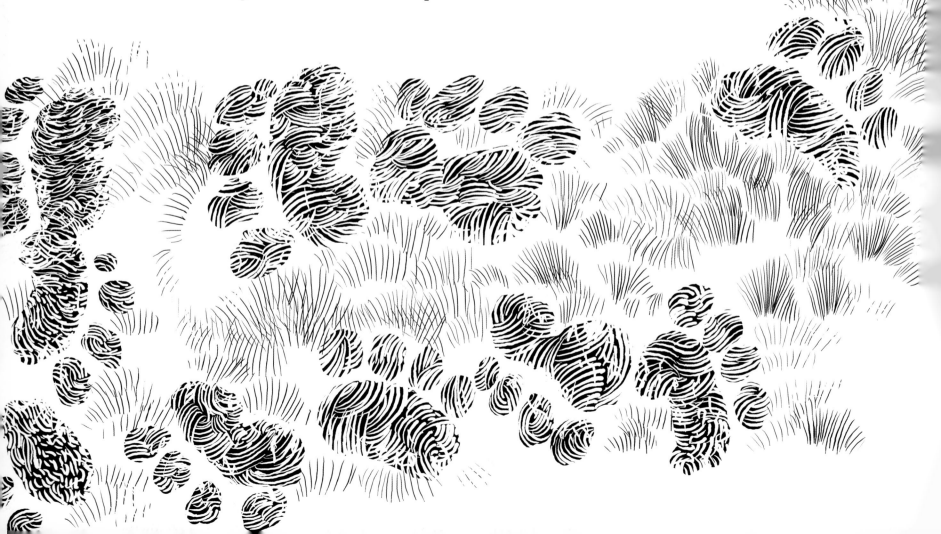

Then they climbed onto the Hodag's spiny back. All night long the Hodag walked backward and forward through the forest. His feet left a trail of giant footprints. Soon there were so many, it was hard to tell if the Hodag was coming or going.

~ *All night long the Hodag walked backward and forward through the forest.* ~

JUST BEFORE SUNRISE, THE HODAG went back to his den. ❖ The lumberjacks made brooms from tree branches and swept away the tracks near the doorway. ❖ "Those animal catchers will never find you now," said Olee Swenson. All day long the animal catchers tried to follow the Hodag's trail. They went around and around until they were dizzy. ❖ "Where is that Hodag?" they asked. "These tracks are fresh. He must be here somewhere."

~ *"Where is that Hodag?"* ~

THE NEXT DAY THE LUMBERJACKS FOUND THE animal catchers digging a deep hole.   ❖   "We're making a Hodag trap," they said. "We'll fill it with blueberry bushes." ❖   The lumberjacks went to work. They were worried. "The Hodag will be really hungry after staying another day in his den," they said. "Now he will be caught for sure."   ❖   "We must think of a way to get rid of those animal catchers for good," said Olee Swenson.   ❖   "How?" asked the men.   ❖   "Perhaps they are not as brave as they think," said Olee Swenson.

~ *"We're making a Hodag trap."* ~

THAT NIGHT THE LUMBERJACKS MET THE HODAG at his den. "Follow us," they said. The Hodag and the lumberjacks walked through the forest to the animal catchers' camp. The lumberjacks hid behind the trees. Then the Hodag stepped into the clearing, stamped his feet, and ROARED. ❖ "Yikes!" yelled the animal catchers as they scrambled out of their tents. They saw a creature with the head of an ox, feet of a bear, back of a dinosaur, and tail of an alligator. "IT'S THE HODAG!" ❖ They jumped up and ran into the forest. The Hodag ran after them. The animal catchers were so scared that they didn't look where they were going. They fell headfirst into the Hodag trap. ❖ "HELP, HELP!" they cried.

OLEE SWENSON AND THE
lumberjacks stepped out from behind
the trees. The animal catchers were stuck
in the bottom of the big hole. ❖ "Watch
out!" shouted the animal catchers. "The Hodag will
eat you." ❖ "No," said Olee Swenson. "The
Hodag is our friend." ❖ "Please tell him not to
hurt us," begged the animal catchers.

"Will you go away and leave him alone?" asked Olee Swenson.

❖ "Yes," they said. ❖ "And you will never come back?" asked Olee Swenson. ❖ "WE PROMISE," they said. "We do not want to see any more of the terrible Hodag."

THE LUMBERJACKS HELPED THE ANIMAL CATCHERS climb out of the hole. Then they gave the blueberry bushes to the Hodag. He ate them all . . .

. . . in three big gulps. The animal catchers packed up
their tents and went back to the city.
Everyone was glad to see them go.

~ *"Thank you," said the Hodag.* ~

"THANK YOU," SAID THE HODAG TO the lumberjacks. ❖ "We were happy to help," they said. They were glad that their friend who had the head of an ox, feet of a bear, back of a dinosaur, and tail of an alligator would stay with them in the forest. It was his home and where he belonged.

FOR CAMPERS AT CAMP BOVEY
past, present, and future
—C.A.

FOR JOHN TATE
always plumb, level, and true
—J.S.

AUTHOR'S NOTE

The first HODAG stories were told in logging camps more than one hundred years ago. I first learned about Olee Swenson and the Hodag as a child, when I went to summer camp in the north woods of Wisconsin. At night, we sat around the campfire and heard tales of a giant beast called the Hodag. As with all tales that pass from one storyteller to the next, the details and exploits of the characters often changed with each telling. *The Terrible Hodag and the Animal Catchers* is an original story based on traditional characters.

THE ARTIST WOULD LIKE TO ACKNOWLEDGE AND THANK

Mr. Bob Jacquart of Stormy Kromer Mercantile for his generous help with historic apparel. A large thanks to Balthazar P. Hodag and his agent, Cornell Chatsworth. Many thanks to Mr. Tim Gillner for his support and ideas on this project, and who, in the end, constructed this book using an ax and a crosscut saw. And, of course, my love to Mrs. Sandford for her saintly patience for more than thirty years. —js

Text copyright © 2006 by Caroline Arnold
Illustrations copyright © 2006 by John Sandford
All rights reserved.

Published by Boyds Mills Press, Inc.
A Highlights Company
815 Church Street
Honesdale, Pennsylvania 18431
Printed in China
Visit our Web site at www.boydsmillspress.com

First edition, 2006
The text of this book is set in 16-point Italian Oldstyle.

10 9 8 7 6 5 4 3 2 1

Publisher Cataloging-in-Publication Data (U.S.)

Arnold, Caroline.
  The terrible Hodag and the animal catchers / by Caroline Arnold ; illustrated by John Sandford.— 1st ed.
       p. cm.
  Summary: When animal catchers come to the forest looking for the scary-looking, but very kindly, Hodag to take him to a zoo, a group of lumberjacks must find a way to protect their friend.
   ISBN 1-59078-166-X (alk. paper)
  [1. Loggers—Fiction. 2. Monsters—Fiction.] I. Sandford, John, 1948-, ill. II. Title.

PZ7.A7346Ter 2006
[Fic]—dc22

2005021141